Backlight

Kanji Hanawa

A former professor of French literature with an interest in human psychology and complex relationships, Hanawa's narratives expose the pressures and challenges of life in Japan.

Hanawa is a master of the short story. He has written several hundred since he published his first collection, *Gurasu no natsu* (*Glass Summer*) to critical acclaim in 1972.

In 1962, after graduating from Tokyo University, where he studied French Literature, he spent several months in Paris, his only stay in the country to whose literature he has dedicated much of his life researching.

Since retiring from academic life (having translated into Japanese 15 novels by some of France's most eminent authors and researching the works of the French poet Arthur Rimbaud), he now lives in Tokyo with his wife and son. He is at last completely free to dedicate himself to his real passion: writing short stories about life in ancient, modern and contemporary Japan.

Two of his novellas have been shortlisted for the prestigious Akutagawa Prize.

Translator: Richard Nathan

Richard Nathan is a Director and Principal of Bosquet Capital and Co-Founder and Director of Red Circle Authors Limited. Prior to this he worked for Kyodo News, the international journal of science *Nature* and the international publisher Macmillan.

Also by Kanji Hanawa in English translation
Compos Mentis

A full publication list of all of Hanawa's work is available from
www.redcircleauthors.com

Backlight

Kanji Hanawa

Translated from the Japanese by
Richard Nathan

Red Circle

Published by Red Circle Authors Limited
First edition 2018
1 3 5 7 9 10 8 6 4 2

Red Circle Authors Limited
Third Floor, 24 Chiswell Street,
London EC1Y 4YX

Red Circle
www.redcircleauthors.com

This book is a work of fiction. The literary perceptions and insights
are based on experience, names, characters and places; and incidents
are either a product of the author's imagination or are used fictionally.
No responsibility for loss caused to any individual or organisation
acting on or refraining from action as a result of the material in this
publication can be accepted by Red Circle Authors or the author.

Design by Aiko Ishida, typesetting by Head & Heart Book Design
Set in Adobe Caslon Pro

ISBN: 978-1-912864-04-1

A catalogue record of this book is available from the British Library.

For my wife, Keiko

Backlight

Day 1

A phone call in the middle of the night, with a request from Toshiko Momose: 'Sorry for inconveniencing you at the beginning of a new academic term, you must be very busy, but could you kindly spare me some of your time?'

Momose was professor emeritus at H University, where Ishida was associate professor of psychology. Momose was still a part-time lecturer, and she was responsible for the course: *Introduction to Psychology.* The two met occasionally to discuss and exchange information.

The context of the request was already of national interest and even starting to be picked up by the international media.

Ishida: 'It's about the missing seven-year-old boy, isn't it?'

No answer was given in the affirmative, but one hardly seemed necessary. The incident alone was enough to send shockwaves through the surrounding peaceful area; there was also the mounting pressure of limited time. This was probably the reason for Momose's rapid speech.

There was a difference between this and most cases of abuse. On first glance this one felt almost pastoral, yet there were certain odd things about it.

It was on the last afternoon of the consecutive May national holidays that three individuals – a father, mother and their daughter – arrived in a small car at a police station on the southern tip of Hokkaido's Oshima Peninsula, having only some ten minutes or so earlier left their eldest child, a boy, A (who shall remain anonymous, along with his family) on the side of a road in the mountains as a punishment, to *discipline* him, so he would be taught a lesson. After a short while they began to feel anxious, and drove back, but A was nowhere to be seen.

The three of them called out for A but there was no response. As they had expected to find him immediately, they panicked, and, according to them, rushed straight to the police station. The police quickly assembled as many people as they could, but it was dusk by then, light rain was falling, and it was cold, so they called it a day and retreated, planning to return the next day with greater numbers, and set up an incident centre and restart the search.

Ishida: 'I imagine, don't you think, they will set up the incident centre at the foot of the mountain?'

Momose: 'They will visit the scene to verify the situation. I am a psychologist, but I'm old, and not so strong on my feet; nor do I have any children myself. So I'm not sure I can be of much use. But I've actually been to take a look, and although they say it's a mountain, it seems more like a nearby hill. The actual location took me by surprise.'

Ishida: 'If you are talking about children, I'm not even married.'

Momose: 'They bring in psychologists even when it is ineffectual, probably so they can

3

demonstrate that they've put together a group of experts.'

Ishida: 'And there's the weather to boot.'

Although the rainy season was approaching, which normally didn't affect Hokkaido, this year there had been unusual and unprecedented weather with persistent pressure patterns.

Additionally, the father's comment about *discipline* and teaching him a lesson also created a sense of unease. The current trend was to bring up children by treating them as if they were your friends; yet these children were often the ones who were constantly causing problems. To put it simply, because raising a child is always such hard work no matter what, there is a tendency to push the responsibility for it onto schools, sports clubs, and the local community.

Momose: 'As for *discipline*, such a method may be extremely harsh. But the majority of children seem to be growing up just fine. The public is hoping that he will be found quickly, with or without these discussions.'

'But why did the family decide to drive up a

mountain in weather like this?'

Momose: 'According to the parents, the holidays were coming to an end, and they were determined to make good on their promise to have a barbecue, even if it was raining. This was a miscalculation. It put A in a bad mood. He was constantly fighting with his sister who is just one year younger than him. That's why they left a child, wearing everyday clothes, behind in the cold rain.'

Ishida: 'Well it wasn't wool, but he had a long-sleeved sweatshirt on, so they thought he'd be all right for a short time. But after some time hypothermia can set in – it creeps up on you.'

Momose: 'Anyway, this isn't for an old person in bad condition, a young person needs to be involved. I'll phone the head of the incident team to let them know. Good luck tomorrow.'

Ishida stayed quiet.

Momose: 'I don't know how effective psychology and child psychology will be in the mountains. I'm staying at the 'XX Inn' not far from Hakodate, and I'll have a good think about all of this. Please could you come over in the evening and update me on the day? The *onsen* (hot spring) is splendid. No. We'll be turning this into another strategic incident centre.'

The one-sided call came to an end, and she hung-up.

Day 2
Overcast, interspersed with rain

Associate Professor Mamoru Ishida was hurriedly awakened and driven to the site, arriving at 2 p.m. The southern end of Hokkaido and Tokyo share a similar longitude, and as Japan's islands are extended and stretch from the east to the west, the mornings in Hokkaido can be light from very early but sunset also arrives relatively quickly.

At the top of a winding, unpaved mountain trail were two large tents at the site where the boy was left. The tent with the rows of steel desks and chairs was the incident centre for meetings with the experts, while in the other tent rice balls and paper cups were laid out across tables.

Seven or eight people from the town hall, as well as A's parents, were sitting there, in an area where the air seemed to hang heavier. Their approach to *discipline*, and their chosen way of teaching him a lesson was still under question, but perhaps they felt obliged to attend, as they were involved. The mayor who had assumed the position of chairperson was announcing changes of personnel. Ishida stood up and introduced himself.

Chairperson: 'The temperature is currently dropping, and the Meteorological Agency is predicting that this trend will continue. Now it is my sincere hope that we make use, at this meeting, of all of our collective knowledge and expertise to enable us to find the boy quickly.'

Just as he was speaking A's mother suddenly announced that she felt unwell, and left with her husband and a nurse. The officials from the town hall, who had been attending despite their busy schedules, also left. Ishida had wanted to ask the parents a question or two, but hesitated and missed his opportunity.

The view of the light green mountainous area should have been visible, but everything was hidden behind a layer of low-lying cloud. The sound of mountain streams and brooks could be heard, but not seen from where they were. Even in mountains that look, at first glance, as tranquil as these, it is impossible to weigh up what terrifying things might be lurking around when the darkness of nightfall completely descends.

Local mountaineer: 'There are small rivers and streams to the left, and to the right is thick forest, which is so dense that even adults would have difficulty walking through it. That's why everyone thinks A must have disappeared near the streams.'

Agawa (a clinical child psychologist): 'So that's why all these people have been returning from around the river.'

In the adjacent tent, men wearing white helmets and *happi* coats (old-fashioned work jackets) muttered amongst themselves as they ate.

Chairperson: 'According to experts and people familiar with these kinds of searches, when individuals are threatened, the mouth goes dry, nothing can be done about it, and most will instinctively go in search of water.'

Agawa: 'It's all about dehydration.'

Forester: 'Neither the mountain nor the valley look inaccessible. But for somebody inexperienced, it's another matter entirely. If you're heading for a place with water, the wilted vegetation looks inviting. But just below there's a cliff that will stop you going further, and if you try to retrace your steps, you will trip on that wilted vegetation, making it impossible to climb back.'

Local mountaineer: 'A little upstream, there's a crossroads where the river and road meet. But I'm confused as to why a seven-year-old boy, walking in light rain, would place so much importance on looking for water.'

Chairperson: 'A new professor of psychology has joined us. On this one point could you give us some insight into how a child might think and act?'

Ishida: 'I can't say anything conclusive, but

it would be linked to how a seven-year-old boy might feel about being left behind, and the boy's personality.'

At that point, a plump, middle-aged woman, A's class teacher, interjected.

Class teacher: 'A's behaviour, grades, social skills, for example, are completely normal. For a second-year student he is big and enjoys sport, and his personality is such that if you meet him he always greets you with a friendly smile.'

Ishida: 'It's standard in Japan to greet people like that. We can't take everything on face value. Sometimes underneath, the child's personality can be unthinkably violent.'

Class teacher: 'That may be true, but I haven't heard negative rumours about this family. When it happened the boy was just having an argument with his sister, wasn't he? His father told him to get out of the car, and he said, "Okay, I will." It seems so lighthearted and mundane. I'm surprised it ended up like this.'

Agawa: 'He's in a fully-fledged rebellious phase.'

Ishida: 'In situations like these, a normal child will burst into tears, scream and shout, or freeze – unable to move, like a hamster being picked up by the scruff of its neck.'

'As of now, 24 hours have elapsed since the disappearance,' the chairperson suddenly declared, looking at his watch.

Ishida: 'It's the sincere children that are a problem. Irresponsible ones just assume that everything will work out as they expected. Even if the father meant it as a sort of game, A probably took it perfectly seriously.'

The smaller search parties were returning in twos and threes. They had been calling out A's name using loudspeakers, then waiting and listening for an answer. They were worried that a lack of response from A might be because he was getting increasingly weak.

Local mountaineer: 'It may seem quiet here, but it is actually filled with sound.'

Agawa: 'That's right. Even small waterfalls constantly emit low frequency sounds. It's a real nuisance.'

The chairperson, who had just pointed out that 24 hours had elapsed, assumed his position as leader of the search parties and started speaking to those returning in a local dialect. The accents of this area are based on the Tohoku dialect spoken on the other side of the straits.

Chairperson: 'It's now getting dark, but those of you from around the area can continue. We'll provide cars for all of you, so please feel free to do what works best for you…'

Ishida: 'Even if it's not possible today, I'd still like to talk with the parents. I am hoping that this can be arranged quickly.'

Chairperson: 'That's perfectly reasonable, but the two of them are in shock. I'd say it is going to be very hard to arrange. It's been impossible to confirm any specific details…'

'We actually approached them a couple of times and I don't think you'll get anywhere with them, even if you do see them,' said Agawa gently, with a wink. 'It's understandable, considering how much they're having to deal with right now.'

Ishida headed to the 'XX Inn' where Momose was staying.

Momose's star pupil, a graduate student by the name of Ai Okubo, was waiting eagerly. Here they bathed in the open-air baths, with their free-flowing spring water, famous amongst travellers for their authentic, traditional Japanese atmosphere. Then they sat down for dinner.

Momose: 'Perhaps this is in poor taste, given the circumstances, but cheers. Here's to exorcising any bad omens from this awful day.'

Beer was poured into Ishida and Okubo's glasses.

Momose (turning the pages of her note-book): 'I've spent a lot of time today mulling things over. And I think that the issue comes down to one point.' As a boy's life was depending on it, her voice was low and reserved.

Ishida: 'That single point... can you elaborate?'

Momose: 'It's the moment the car drives off, after A got out. It's not as if the family really gets along that badly, and the father said that it was all done in the spirit of a game. So, when the car drives off down the mountain, the question is, how did everything appear to A?'

Ishida: 'Ms. Okubo, what might you say the car symbolises?'

Still holding her glass of beer up to her mouth, Okubo glanced at Momose.

Okubo: 'A symbol of home, no?'

Momose: 'The car means family, it is a condensed version of home. So in that instant, he saw very clearly his relationship with the family. Even though, normally it wouldn't be completely clear.'

Ishida: 'So just from a quick glance through the car window, he thinks he's seen his position within the family. He thinks even if I am not there, they're happy, or they're happier without me. Even if he believed that they'd come back to get him quickly, that momentary impression would have never left him. Is that what you mean?'

Okubo: 'In the toy section of department

stores, parents often say "I will leave you here" to children making a fuss.'

Ishida: 'There's a vast difference between a place like that and the middle of the mountains. Something entirely at odds with the playful mood A's family were enjoying must have occurred.'

Momose: 'It's that single moment that determines everything that happened afterwards. How did the family appear as it was happening? Were they in good spirits, laughing, chatting away? It may have broken A's perception of something being a game.'

Ishida: 'Consider those words: "Get out of the car" and "Maybe I will get out." This exchange became a tit-for-tat. I wanted to investigate this idea further, but both parents seem on the verge of crumbling, like sandcastles on the beach.'

Momose: 'I don't think the parents are seeing things clearly. The precise time frame of returning quickly still remains unclear. The difference between "shortly" and "quickly" is significant when a car is concerned, and from A's perspective, I'd think, this difference was even greater.'

Day 3
Dense fog, cold temperatures, cold rain

The statement compiled by Momose and Ishida was circulated to the chairperson and the others, but with questionable levels of comprehension. As a child was concerned, the media was showing some self-control. Even so, overall opinion was shifting; it was being taken much more seriously. More and more people were calling for a search of the greatest magnitude possible, even if hastily executed, with the largest number of people available. As a result there were 300 people in total, both locals and non-locals, forming small search parties and heading into the area. Despite this, there was no positive news.

'It has now been 48 hours,' the chairperson announced gravely. There could be no doubt now that A would be freezing cold. In contrast to the returning search parties, covered in dirt and leaves, the 'discussion only' attendees of the conference may well have been viewed now as rather useless. As people returned, the chairperson remarked, 'It's quite chilly around here. Perhaps it would be better to be on standby somewhere else contactable.'

This was an indication that things were escalating. If A had, for example, fallen into water, the end would have come swiftly and definitively. But for any other scenario, the situation was complex and not a single thing could be predicted with any degree of accuracy. It only went to show what little impact the search was having. Agawa walked towards Ishida.

Agawa: 'Are you aware that the colder the climate, the larger the animals living there tend to be? Like Asian black bears, brown bears, polar bears. I don't know if you've seen, but today the search teams began carrying thin poles to prod around the area. Whatever's going on, it's awful.'

Ishida: 'Are you saying that the search objectives have been changed?'

They talked back and forth, passing the time, calming their mounting frustration and washing down their feelings of exasperation with tea.

In the evening, Ishida invited Agawa to join him at Momose's inn.

Momose: 'Ah, that's how it works. I wasn't aware that the larger the body the greater the resistance to cold. With A's body that's a considerable disadvantage. If you indulge me and follow this reasoning... it might explain why old people, like me, are so hot-tempered.' She laughed.

Momose, who was meeting Agawa for the first time, dispensed with the usual words of greeting and leaned her head forwards with unashamed naked curiosity.

Agawa: 'Ah, a mathematical puzzle in lieu of a greeting.' He chuckled. 'Intriguing. Essentially, even as the volume of an object increases in size the surface area doesn't increase proportionally. If you attach two six-sided dice together, you double the volume, but because two faces are joined together, you only have the total surface area of ten sides. In a cold climate, having a high ratio of surface area to body size and a proportionally large body surface from which heat can be lost is always a disadvantage. Compared to an adult, A will also be at a significant disadvantage.'

The solution to this somewhat perplexing problem helped lighten the mood. Agawa commented on the wonderful atmosphere the open-air baths had, and then they began a dinner with different kinds of dishes of seasonal bamboo shoots.

Ishida: 'I have re-examined all of the psychological aspects of this case. Whether A was left behind for a few seconds or a few minutes makes a really big difference. At today's specialists' meeting we distributed a statement about this, but I'm not sure it was fully understood.'

Momose: 'What he saw at that moment is a very hard thing for us to understand.'

Ishida: 'It might have been strangers he saw, or it could have been "demons".'

Agawa: '"Demons"? That's unexpected. Outwardly they may have all looked like angels. A group of smiling angels.'

Ishida: 'That's rich coming from a clinical psychologist. But actually, this is an extreme situation.'

As Ishida spoke he felt as if he had been hit in the back.

Momose (consulting her notebook): 'Since I couldn't go to the mountains, I've spent hour after hour thinking this through. The symbolism of being left behind. It seems rare. Rare, but perhaps it really isn't so extraordinary for humans and all creatures.'

Ishida: 'Ah, flying the nest and taking leave from one's parents?'

Momose: 'That's just one example. Animals leave their offspring to fend for themselves, and only the tough ones survive. So even siblings can become "demons" that have to be fought. If you break physically or mentally under pressure, you will inevitably end up dead.'

Ishida: 'If that is the case, it was a subconscious gambit by the parents, creating a stage for them to act out abandonment.'

Okubo: 'Sea turtles are the same. In order to live, newborn turtles have to crawl by themselves to the sea, under their own strength.'

Momose: 'It doesn't end there. There are many more ways of being left behind. There are different types of "demons". A contemporary can get promoted, somebody younger can outpace you, a relative can be happier. The people closest to you are the ones most likely to become your demon. You may not let it show on the surface but inside things may not be that calm, on either side, and all of a sudden one of you has become the demon.'

Agawa: 'It happens. Maybe abandonment, and the fear of it, is the force that powers our hearts – its own "libido", if you will.'

'I would assume that when a car was used to abandon a child, things would be different and it would be a grey area. There's even a song about a car's tail light. The car belongs to a lover who has just broken up with someone and the tail light flickers just as it turns a corner and disappears,' Okubo added, as she refilled everyone's beer glasses.

Momose: 'The father did it to A meaning to teach him that sometimes things like this happen in life. But A only saw it as callous, and in revenge wanted to do something to upset his father, so he decided to disappear heading into the bush instead of in the direction of the mountain rivers.'

Ishida: 'That does sound logical. Initially, A must have heard his family calling but didn't respond. Then, when it was the locals calling, he must have thought he had missed his chance to come out, so he went into deeper hiding, and before he knew it no longer knew how to find the way back.'

Agawa: 'I have to say, I'm a little startled by everybody's analysis. Initially, when the incident centre considered the mountain streams, the worry was that A would die quickly. If he slipped and fell from a rock in the river and died from shock, the river would then carry his dead body out to sea. Such an awful thing had to be prevented. The scenario that he might have gone into the mountains never came up.'

Ishida: 'Yes, but we gave them a report detailing the opposite just this morning.'

Okubo: 'I suppose that's what they mean by, in one ear and out the other.'

Day 4
Weather unchanged, lack of sunlight exacerbating conditions

Issues surrounding the curriculum at the start of the academic year meant that Ishida had no choice but to show his face at his university. It was only in the evening that he eventually managed to head off to Momose and the others to pick up on the main points of the psychological analysis discussed the previous evening. As Okubo said, in one ear and out the other, but it was confirmed that Agawa had submitted their report to the investigation team, as requested.

Earlier, following a complete review of the situation, the local government belatedly expanded the search area so it fanned out to a much greater area from the point where the child was left behind. From multiple different locations in the vicinity people headed towards the summit. A multifold increase in the number of individuals making up the search parties was made and people were released in a full frontal assault using an infantry-type, human sea attack strategy. The search teams previously involved were also incorporated in the new approach. As soon as Agawa arrived and was ready the meeting started.

Agawa: 'I asked around, but if the entire mountainous area is factored in, the area is ten times as large, making it impossible to estimate where to start and how far the search party should go.'

Okubo: 'They do have police dogs, don't they?'

Agawa: 'I heard that when there is running water, a dog's sense of smell can't be relied on.'

Ishida: 'Even dogs must hate damp thickets.'

Momose: 'The clouds and rain. That, I think, is the key. If there is good weather you can see the summit and understand why you might head for it. If it goes on like this, the total lack of a sense of direction is going to just continue. They can't use helicopters or drones, and introducing a larger number of people is good, but could create a knock-on secondary disaster.'

Agawa: 'The unusual weather, I have to say, is having a real bruising effect. With a group of others I entered a thicket wearing work overalls, and it was immediately obvious what a difficult business it is. The shrubbery is dense and overgrown. It makes you wonder if a child's feet would actually reach the ground below.'

Momose: 'You know, when people familiar with the mountains enter the wilds, they often look for a branch that stands out, and break it to mark their tracks. It's useful on the way back. It's called a *shiori*, a folded branch, just like the word for bookmark. It is written differently but is pronounced the same. But that's probably not something a child brought up in the city would think to do.'

Okubo: 'Is the origin of bookmark really folded branch?'

Momose: 'You know, much of the basis of psychology is folktales and fairytales. Would you be interested in talking about this further?

European folktales from the Middle Ages are famous from the 18th or 19th century collections of stories by the Grimm brothers, but you find plenty of other similar stories about abandonment in many other countries. If I'm not mistaken there are also Perrault's tales, from 17th-century France, I think. I am not sure if that is right, my memory isn't that good these days.'

Ishida: 'I imagine abandonment in Europe during the Middle Ages must have happened often. Every time there was a famine. I remember a tale about a woodcutter and his wife facing starvation who are overheard by their youngest child discussing abandoning their children in the woods. The next morning the youngest child gets up early, fills his pockets with pebbles collected from a dry riverbed and then carefully drops them on route. In the depths of the forest, when the right opportunity arises the parents rush off, but the children use the pebbles to find their way back.'

Okubo: 'I remember now. But what a sad story.'

Ishida: 'Yes, the parents gloss over it, pretending nothing happened, but the next time there's a famine the youngest child doesn't have time to pick up pebbles and so used breadcrumbs leftover from breakfast instead, which the birds ate. So they couldn't find their way back. And even though all kinds of things happen, they are saved time and time again by the common sense of the youngest kid.'

Momose: 'Europe back then was covered in dense forest. Small plots were cleared out creating pastures and farms. But in parallel, as diets shifted to grains and breads, the number of climate-change related famines increased. Instead of depending on the countryside and whatever it produced, a single-crop strategy of wheat was adopted. The scars of these past disasters run deep. Even today, I am convinced, people in Western Europe haven't completely forgotten. I am sure that's why this, a child being left behind abandoned, has made such an impression and has been picked up by the media.'

Agawa: 'So is that why, on this rare occasion, they've picked up the story enthusiastically?'

Ishida: 'News from Japan doesn't travel and hardly ever gets reported abroad. It is almost as if Japan's winds do not travel far.'

Momose: 'Legends and folktales, even fairytales, are part of the collective subconscious of each generation. At the same time, they evolve to fit the times. As many of the original Grimm brothers' tales are extremely cruel, and would embarrass most Germans, the stories have been rewritten. In the original *Snow White* the villain is actually the real mother – the biological mother – who has since been substituted by a stepmother.'

Agawa: 'There is a theory that it's the origin of the stereotype about stepmothers being cruel. Rewriting of folktales, legends, and their misuse began, didn't it, when the Nazis used old myths to frighten and influence people?'

Ishida: 'Well, in this case Japan is no different. The number of similar cruel stories are vast. The origin of the term *kamikakushi*, "spirited away", is said to be unknown, but in the end, it's all about the same thing. Killing children in times of famine.'

As Ishida finished, Okubo refilled everyone's glasses with beer.

Momose: 'Whenever things get uncomfortable, the causes become obscured. I read somewhere that from a very young age, Kunio Yanagita, probably the most knowledgeable individual in Japan about folklore and these sorts of things often thought: "I am going to be spirited away", but perhaps he had this premonition because he had been a small and sweet boy. I have no idea what A is like.'

Okubo finished refilling everybody's beer glasses and laughed.

Agawa: 'I don't know much about Yanagita, but if you look at that famous photograph of the good-natured old man, you do get the sense that maybe when he was very young, different spirits from the mountains, rivers, or forests – from another realm – might have been right there beside him.'

Momose: 'The reason why Western countries are so interested in A is, as I've said already, because the act of abandoning a child in the forest reminds them of Europe in the Middle Ages, and is also, in fact, indicative of the type of original sin that can't be forgotten. I'd like to say that cruel folktales like this don't exist in Japan, but then again, the concealed killing of children has obviously happened in societies everywhere.'

Day 5
Weather conditions unchanged

Even though the number of people deployed had been increased massively, the progress of the search hadn't changed. Emotions were shifting and rising from impatience to desperation.

At the conference in the evening, the attendees continued the discussion initiated previously.

Momose: 'Earlier I was talking about original sin, but I read something about the difference between child behaviour in America and Japan that really surprised me. When a child is shut out, left alone outside of home, a Japanese child will stay glued to the spot, cry and apologise, because it is absolutely unbearable for the child.'

Ishida: 'Is it different overseas?'

Momose: 'Apparently, it's different. In the same situation, a child over there doesn't feel restricted but free. They quickly just head off somewhere to play. So it's not an effective form of punishment.'

Agawa: 'But, if you actually do it, it seems very dangerous. It could be neglect. There could be an abduction or a serious injury.'

Momose: 'Exactly because of that, the fear of a potential crime stops parents from locking out their child. So, the punishment is actually prohibiting them from leaving the house and going out. Anyway, it seems the concept of "freedom" in the West is the opposite to that in Japan.'

Ishida: 'In Japan we're actually much more dependent on family. I suppose this is an after-effect of the long history of people protecting their place and position in society.'

Momose: 'Until now this difference in behaviour is thought to have been chiefly cultural, but research papers show that recently hypotheses are being generated that suggest there may even be differences in DNA.'

Agawa: 'It's no longer cultural theory. It's deeper.'

Momose: 'Exactly. In the 15th and 16th centuries, the Age of Discovery, if you wanted to make a name for yourself, you set out to cross dangerous oceans. Despite the risks and dangers, a huge number of people have made groundbreaking discoveries. In Japan, in similar situations, it was hard to tread your own path. Those who left the country were prohibited from re-entering. It's interesting that just as Japan was curling up and shrinking into itself, St. Francis Xavier suddenly appeared. He came from the Basque region, sandwiched between France and Spain. He was a tough child from farming stock who could easily deal with isolation. He arrived here after a long and arduous voyage. The Basque people are notorious for being headstrong and resilient in this sort of way. Later, when the frontier on the American continent was opened up, people who had gone there from the Basque region moved across without hesitation.

'There is no doubt that Xavier did a lot, but you can't beat the Japanese. After listening to a sermon, one farmer apparently stood up and asked: "If your God is omnipotent then why did he not send you to us earlier? It's too late now, everyone's already decided on their beliefs." Apparently, it annoyed Xavier and left him speechless.'

Agawa: 'As he didn't have an answer, it is not really that surprising that the number of believers in Christianity in Japan is still less than one percent. I am sure that is the sort of question that should never be asked, not only in Japan, but in any country.'

Momose: 'Xavier took the southern passage to Japan. There weren't any Western controlled colonies yet, so he must have only encountered stubborn hostility. Japan was the first place he was welcomed, and invited to dinner. This hospitality continued across the entire country. Xavier may have feared that Christianity would ruin the nation, as he wrote to a clergyman friend saying that he should not come and that it was better if he stayed far away, since Japan had the worst weather, and its inhabitants displayed perverse attitudes, like no other country.

'He must have anticipated that when an inward-looking culture collides with an outward-facing one, it can lead to disaster. It's actually what happened to the Inca and the Mayan civilizations. Japan has an enormous neighbour, China, and is by no means an entirely isolated culture, but there is something about the Japanese character that sets it apart.'

Ishida: 'Looked at in that way, the boy A is unusual in that he sensed a moment of "freedom" and bolted in an act of outrageous rebellion against those treating him like that. A Xavier type, perhaps, or rebellious behaviour? Well, no one knows about that now, or thought that such a type existed and that's what has caused all this commotion.'

Momose: 'Instead of responding and being obedient and docile, at first with the parents and then later when the initial search parties were in place, he decided to react and rebel, and as a prank, in defiance, left the scene.'

Ishida: 'He saw his "demons" in the car window. Is that his reaction?'

Momose: 'Evidently. At first he just hid, but even with a child's legs, you can go far. He probably thought the mountains would be easy. And all of a sudden he lost his bearings and was completely at sea, surrounded by bush, with no broken branches or pebbles marking the route to help him find his way back.'

Agawa: 'It's certainly true that at the top of a mountain when it rains it feels like being in the clouds. Even a long-sleeve shirt and long trousers will start getting wet and damp. Clothes, like a wet towel, cling to the skin. And before you know it, hypothermia slowly sets in.'

Momose: 'You're right. Although, if you're wearing another layer, a knitted sweater or something like that, it could probably be another story.'

Day 6
No changes to the weather

In a completely unexpected turn of events, things came to an abrupt, but happy conclusion.

Reports arrived from one of the small search parties that had crossed from the centre to the other side of the woods in the cold rain, that 'a young child in good spirits has been located.' The reports were greeted with cheers by members of the search teams, who were now 1,000 people in number. The cheers and smiles were tempered with the exhaustion that everyone felt.

According to those who found him, in an opening cleared of all vegetation, near a peak, deep in the mountains, they came across three buildings, rusty-brown in colour, that looked like military warehouses. Since there were no paths leading to the area (otherwise A would descend himself), the only option for extraction was by helicopter. Nevertheless, the Self-Defense Forces (SDF) hadn't said anything about them.

Of the buildings, the lock on the one in the centre was broken. Just to be sure, someone entered, and there was the young boy who walked out on steady feet. He nodded silently when asked, 'Are you A?' A pile of thick mats apparently for camping or battlefield hospitals, were stored inside.

Somehow A had pulled out two mats, which were very heavy from the pile and had been sleeping sandwiched between the two of them. He had put out his wet clothes to dry, which he was wearing at the time of his discovery, showed no signs of hypothermia and was mentally sharp. Although he was probably hungry, he was still strong physically too. Fortunately, at the entrance of the warehouse there was a tap connected to a well from which he drank to quench his thirst.

The doctor who examined him (who wasn't Agawa) concluded that snuggling between

the mats restricted movement, protected him
from the cold and stopped exhaustion setting
in. And the almost miraculous presence of
water had saved him. After being briefly
hospitalised, where he was put on a drip and
received some other medical treatment, the
visible after-effects from living in isolation in
the mountains had disappeared.

The police considered investigating the
parents further for parental abandonment, but
since the entire family felt incredibly guilty
and pleaded to be left alone, and there was no
indication of or rumours of child abuse, the
police took no further action. Similarly, requests
from journalists for interviews were limited. The
day quickly drew to an end without the details
of what happened being known.

In the afternoon, Ishida visited Momose
at the inn. Agawa, had arrived a few moments
before and had already left, having asked for his
'best wishes' to be passed on to everyone.

Ishida: 'I'm sorry but I also have to go and
make my way back to the university, but it's

amazing, don't you think, that a child could walk five kilometres like that deep into the woods?'

Momose: 'It's just like something out of Hansel and Gretel, even the part about hiding in a warehouse. But if his reason for hiding was, as we theorised, no matter how many times the search party called out his name he probably wasn't the sort of child who would just come out and say, "I'm here, I am sorry!" He is headstrong. To him the loudspeakers may have even sounded like beaters in a hunt.'

Ishida: 'You're right, it wasn't in him to simply and obediently step out. I am sure he heard the calls. I don't want to mix things up again, but if there weren't really any problems with how the family got along, then why, on a simple matter like this of being taught a lesson, did it lead to the exchange beginning with the parent's order for their son to "Get-out" followed by the boy's retaliation: "Okay, I will"? It's really strange.'

Momose: 'What goes on inside people, inside a family, within society, even the inner workings of a nation, they are all peculiar things that are difficult to understand, and always bound to be controversial and unexpected.'

Ishida: 'That must be it!'

Momose: 'Because you've assisted in an official capacity, you will be compensated at a daily rate, which you will certainly get. Of course, it won't be anywhere near enough. I'll let you know in due course. I've taken a liking to this inn, so I'm going to stay on for two, or maybe three days and take it easy. But I will certainly give the upcoming lecture.'

Okubo: 'I am going to stay with Professor Momose.'

Just like that, and not without some regret about leaving 'XX Inn's' open-air baths and its atmosphere behind, Ishida boarded the express train for Sapporo. It was an odd emergency that ended without incident, creating a sense of relief that finally allowed him to relax. On top of that, he felt dirt-tired and his whole body started to ache.

He gazed at the scenery sweeping past the train window. The stubborn bad weather didn't look likely to change, and this irregular climate seemed to be affecting the whole world.

Are things really so visible?

As he dozed off, Ishida thought back over the sequence of events. The theories about *discipline*, child counselling, educational institutions, responsible individuals and guardians and, ultimately, the entire world. It was all incredibly confused. But, putting that aside, one of the theories that Momose let slip helped stimulate and loosen Ishida's consciousness, which suddenly started working in overdrive.

Yes, it was the image of a family leaving one of its members behind. If this was just your typical conventional disciplinary action, A would have probably sat quietly for ten or twenty minutes, and waited for the family to return. And once they had, there would be some kind of basic reconciliation, no matter how awkward. But somehow a gear jammed, and it didn't happen, leading to this ridiculous incident becoming a major event.

Ishida briefly glanced at the sky above through the train window. The sun shone down almost compassionately. Perhaps, the bad weather was finally coming to an end. What was it about this case that kept on evading Ishida, throughout the search, lurking in the background? There was something he couldn't figure out. This strong sense of confusion, was it about him, something inside him?

The memory wasn't lucid enough to recall exactly when it had happened. In truth, when he was a child, he hadn't been particularly well behaved... Certainly not when compared to his older sister... As the wished-for son, there were enormous expectations. He didn't exactly have the best grades and he sometimes snuck out of home, without saying anything, hiding, worrying his mother.

Yes, at what age would that have happened...? When, by pure coincidence, he learnt his actual position within the family. His parents and his sister walked right past where he was hiding. The three of them looked so happy and were having fun, joking around, in a manner he had never seen before. Even his father, who was always stern and strict, was smiling away.

What was this all about and how did it happen? Basically, his family were perfectly happy in his absence. He had a hunch that, if they were all having such a good time, he'd run away and stay away, giving them something to really worry about. In short, if he wasn't around... but no... if this family were some place where he wasn't, they would suddenly become like this. Was it really so much fun if he wasn't included? That's how he felt and he ran off, because just for a short time he wanted to make them incredibly worried. Because for him, this was when the whole world started to be unfair.

And he, the individual who had been observing the search for A, was actually the same child. And now, armed with everything he had studied, and from analysing A, and his own deductive reasoning, he could make his own recommendations. In short, he looked down on everything from above at a distance. As an undergraduate, a graduate student, a professor, because that was just the way he went about his work.

But this time, that wasn't the case. When he had to act as an associate professor, maybe the strange uneasy feeling he had was in all likelihood because he could see A's hidden, distinctly un-Japanese qualities? Taking a safe bird's-eye view was easy. But to see others on an equal footing, you needed to place yourself in an entirely different position.

Perhaps, he had seen the same "demons" as A. No it was more accurate to say the child had thought he had seen them. Wasn't it he, himself, who was continuously shining a light on others to prove something? He was actually uncomfortable with his own position and because of that he sought to observe himself using a spotlight from above. The truth was,

there was something much larger, a backlight.
And like a moth in blazing light, his true shape
and colours could now be made out.

(From Mamoru Ishida's case memo, substantive points only)

'I have admired, the Akutagawa Prize-nominated Hanawa's literary style for a long time. Each time he is nominated, I recommend him. And I am delighted that he continues to write at the same prize-winning level.'

Shohei Ooka, novelist and winner of the Mystery Writers of Japan Award, as well as the Noma, Asahi and Yomiuri Prizes

'The universal and timeless theme of this thought-provoking and intriguing story is one of identity and self-worth. It cleverly touches on the realms of family dynamics, child psychology and even the influence of legends and fairytales on the collective consciousness – whether inside or outside Japan. And as the story closes we come to fully understand our protagonist's initial cynicism and reluctance to take part in the search for the missing boy in the first place, as this perfectly structured tale comes full circle.'

Alex Pearl, author of *Sleeping with the Blackbirds*

'He writes with a surreal style, similar to how I do on occasion, which I find very interesting and stimulating. But what makes me really happy is that he does it so much better than I do.'

Makoto Shiina, author of *Gaku Monogatari*

Red Circle Minis

Original, Short and Compelling Reads

Red Circle Minis is a series of short captivating books by Japan's finest contemporary writers that brings the narratives and voices of Japan together as never before. Each book is a first edition written specifically for the series and is being published in English first.

The book covers in the series draw on traditional Japanese motifs and colours found in Japanese building, paper, garden and textile design. Everything, in fact, that is beautiful and refined, from kimonos to zen gardens and everything in between. The mark included on the covers incorporates the Japanese character *mame* meaning 'bean', a word that has many uses and connotations including all things miniature and adorable. The colour used on this cover is known as *haiume*.

 Red Circle

Showcasing Japan's Best Creative Writing

Red Circle Authors Limited is a specialist publishing company that publishes the works of a carefully selected and curated group of leading contemporary Japanese authors.

For more information on Red Circle, Japanese literature, and Red Circle authors, please visit:
www.redcircleauthors.com